This Book Belongs to:

Mickey's Young Readers Library

VOLUME

12

Pluto and the Big Race

© MCMXC **The Walt Disney Company.**

Developed by The Walt Disney Company in conjunction with Nancy Hall, Inc.

Story by Mary Carey/Activities by Thoburn Educational Enterprises, Inc.

This book may not be reproduced or transmitted in any form or by any means.

ISBN 1-885222-45-9

Advance Publishers Inc., P.O. Box 2607, Winter Park, FL. 32790

Printed in the United States of America

0987654321

"Say—that's a great box car!" Goofy said. He grinned at Morty and Ferdie. "I had one just like that when I was your age," he told them.

The boys were in Mickey's drive, giving their new box car the finishing touches. "We made it ourselves," Morty said. He sounded very proud.

"We're going to take it for a test run pretty soon," Ferdie added.

Pluto pushed close and sniffed at the oil can.

"Pluto!" Ferdie cried. "You'll get oil all over everything!"

"Aren't you going to paint your car before you take it out?" asked Goofy. "I painted the one I had. It was red, and it had silver wheels."

"We'll paint it blue once we've saved up enough money for the paint," Ferdie said.

"We're naming our car the *Blue Streak*," Morty added.

"Good name!" Goofy nodded, as he walked away.

Pluto watched Goofy go. Then he turned to
Morty and Ferdie. The boys were still busy with the
car. But maybe they weren't too busy to play ball
with him! He ran and got his ball. Then he barked.

"Later, Pluto," Morty said. Then he tightened a wheel on the car.

Pluto brought the ball over to the box car. He sat up and begged.

"We're busy now," said Ferdie. "We're doing important stuff. Go play someplace else for a while—okay?"

Pluto didn't know what to do next. What can a dog do when no one will play with him?

He can take a nap! And that is exactly what Pluto decided to do. He found a nice shady spot on the porch. He lay down there in front of the doorway. Pluto closed his eyes. For a few minutes he heard the birds sing in the trees. Then he did not hear them. He was asleep.

Suddenly the door banged open. Mickey dashed
out, and he tripped right over Pluto!
Pluto yelped and came wide awake.

Mickey tumbled down the steps. For a second he just sat and frowned at Pluto.

Pluto hung his head. He waited for Mickey to tell him it was all right. Instead Mickey said, "Silly dog, sleeping in the doorway."

Mickey got up and brushed himself off. "Next time you need a nap, go sleep in your doghouse," Mickey told Pluto.

He went down the drive and stopped for a moment to tell the boys how nice their car looked. Then he walked down the street.

Pluto did not try to follow Mickey. It was not the right time to follow Mickey. Instead, Pluto got his ball and started up the street. He wanted to find someone who would play ball with him.

Pluto passed by Donald Duck's house. But Donald was not out watering his grass.

Pluto passed by Daisy Duck's house. But Daisy was not out taking care of her roses.

At last Pluto came to the house where Minnie Mouse lived. He stopped. He went and scratched at Minnie's door. Perhaps she would come out and play with him.

Suddenly Pluto saw a bush by Minnie's house shaking. Something was hiding in the bushes. Could it be a robber? Or was some wild animal about to jump out at Minnie? Nothing would leap out at Minnie! Not while Pluto was around to stop it! Pluto growled and jumped at the bush.

But there was no robber, no wild animal. There was only a tiny bird who had stopped to rest.

The bird gave a CHIRP! and flapped her wings.

Minnie looked out her door and said, "Oh, Pluto, how could you scare such a pretty little thing?"

But Pluto hadn't known that the thing in the bush was a bird. Poor Pluto! Everything was going so wrong for him today.

Pluto started to walk away, but Minnie went after him. "I think I'll just walk you home," she said. "That way you'll be sure to stay out of trouble."

Pluto trotted meekly beside Minnie as she led him back to Morty and Ferdie.

"I don't know what's gotten into Pluto," Minnie
told the boys. "He was chasing a poor little bird
outside my house."

"Pluto, did you really do that?" Morty asked.

"I'm surprised at you, Pluto," said Ferdie.

Then Morty and Ferdie turned away. They were
ready to try out their car at last.

Pluto followed the boys to a hill near the house.
He watched Morty get behind the wheel of the
car. He saw Ferdie push the car, then hop in.
    Away the two went down the hill! Now that
looked like fun to Pluto. He raced after the car,
barking like mad.

Going up the hill again was not such fun. The
boys had to push the car every step of the way.
Pluto decided to ride, and he jumped into the car.
"Pluto, get out!" said Morty. "You're too heavy!"
"We can't push with you in the car!" said
Ferdie. Pluto didn't understand. He couldn't do
anything right today. So he took his ball and walked
away. He would go to the park and play by himself.

In the park, Pluto met a little boy who patted his head. "Good doggie," said the little boy.

Pluto put his ball down and barked.

The boy picked up the ball and threw it. At last! Someone who wanted to play ball.

But the ball landed on top of a shed. Pluto could not reach it. The boy couldn't reach it either. "Too bad," said the boy, and he walked away.

There was only one thing to do. Pluto headed for home. Surely the boys were tired of the car by now. Surely they would come and get the ball.

But Morty and Ferdie were not quite done with the car. However, when Pluto barked and headed for the park, they followed. Pluto led them to the shed. He barked at the roof. The boys saw the problem.

"Okay, Pluto, we see the ball," said Ferdie.
"We'll get it for you," Morty told him.
Morty climbed on Ferdie's shoulders. He
grabbed the ball and threw it to Pluto. Then he
jumped down.

"Hey, look!" Ferdie pointed to a sign near the shed. "Big Box-Car Race," said the sign. "All Drivers Invited, 2 P.M. Today. Blackberry Hill."

"A box-car race!" cried Morty. "Today? And here we are with a brand-new, fast-as-lightning box car!"

"What are we waiting for?" asked Ferdie. "Let's go!"

Pluto and the boys raced back to Mickey's house. They had left the box car in the drive, but now it was not there. There was nothing in the drive now but an oil can and some tools.

"Where'd it go?" Morty asked, looking around.

"Maybe Uncle Mickey came home and put it in the garage," offered Ferdie.

But the box car was not in the garage.

"Maybe it rolled out of the drive and down the street," said Morty.

They looked toward the bottom of the street, but the car was not there.

"Could anyone be mean enough to take our box car?" wondered Morty.

"Maybe we should call the police," said Ferdie.

Then the boys saw Pluto acting strangely. He sniffed the ground. He ran up and down. Then he sniffed some more.

"What are you doing, Pluto?" asked Morty.

Pluto lifted his head and barked. He pointed with his nose as if to say, "This way!" Then he barked again.

"Oh, that's funny," laughed Morty. "Pluto thinks he's a detective dog. He's going to track a runaway box car."

"Do you think he really could?" asked Ferdie.

"Aw, come on now," Morty laughed again. "He's just a plain dog, not a detective or a hunting dog. But don't worry, Pluto, we love you anyway. You can stop pretending now," Morty said.

But Pluto did not stop. He ran farther up the street. He barked and barked.

"Let's give him a chance," said Ferdie. "He wants us to follow him. Maybe he does know something after all."

"Well, okay," agreed Morty. "We have nothing to lose."

The boys trotted down the street after Pluto. They passed Donald's house and Daisy's house. They passed Minnie's house, too. They went all the way to the house where Goofy lived.

There stood Goofy with the box car. The car looked wonderful. It was painted a bright blue!

"Gawrsh! You caught me!" said Goofy. "I wanted to surprise you. I remembered I had some fast-drying blue paint. I'm almost done. I'll just put the name on—*Blue Streak,* like you wanted."

"Thanks, Goofy. But we don't have time," said Morty.

"We have a box-car race to win," cried Ferdie.

"Better get going then," Goofy agreed.

The boys started out of the driveway with the box car. Pluto stood beside Goofy and watched. He did not try to go along. He did not want to do anything wrong. Suddenly the boys stopped and looked back.

"Hey, Pluto, come on, boy!" called Morty.

"Stick with us, Pluto!" said Ferdie.

Pluto scooted after Morty and Ferdie. He followed them to Blackberry Hill. The racers were lined up there. The race was about to start.

"Come on, Pluto," cried Ferdie. "Hop on!"

"Be our mascot!" said Morty.

Pluto gave a glad yelp. He jumped into the car.

"Ready! Get set! Go!" shouted the starter.

Down the hill they went. In seconds, Morty and Ferdie pulled ahead of the others. Pluto felt the wind blowing his ears.

The boys streaked across the finish line.

"We did it!" shouted Ferdie. "We won! We won!"

Morty hugged Pluto. "You brought us luck, Pluto. You're a winner too."

The judges awarded a gold trophy to the boys.

"Does your box car have a name?" asked one of the judges.

"We were going to call it the *Blue Streak,* but maybe we won't," said Morty. "Maybe *Pluto's Pride* would be a better name."

Morty looked at Ferdie. "What do you think?" he asked.

"I think it's a great idea!" announced Ferdie. "If it weren't for Pluto, we wouldn't have won the race. Why, we wouldn't have even known there was a box-car race!"

"It's true," Morty added, "who would have guessed that Pluto would save the day?"

Pluto wagged his tail hard. He was happy. He had finally done something right that day!

Think About It

Pluto Strikes Again!

In this story, Pluto gets in everyone's way! Look carefully at each picture. For each one, tell who it was that Pluto upset. Do you remember in which order these four things happened?

After your child does the activities in this book, refer to the *Young Readers Guide* for the answers to these activities and for additional games, activities, and ideas.

Pluto's Very Bad Day

In the beginning of the story, Pluto wasn't having a very good day. Do you remember having a very bad day? Tell what happened to you. By the end of the story, Pluto's day had gotten a lot better. Explain why. Then think about how your very bad day might have been made better.

Fun With Words

Detective Pluto

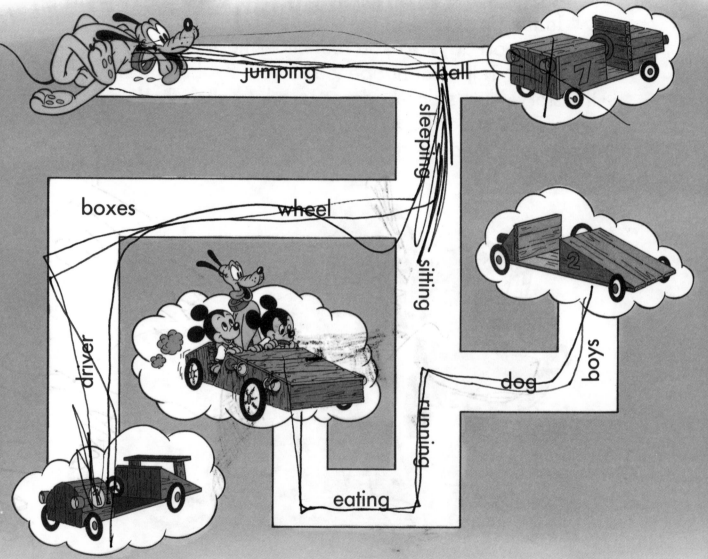

jumping

ball

sleeping

sitting

boxes

wheel

driver

running

dog

boys

eating

Help Pluto find Morty and Ferdie's boxcar. With your finger, trace the path that contains the action words.

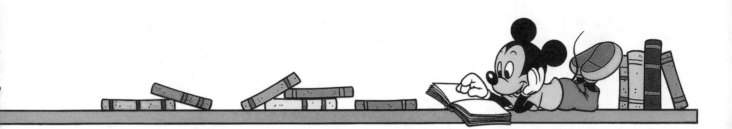

What Can Pluto Do?

Point to the *action* word that best describes each picture of Pluto.

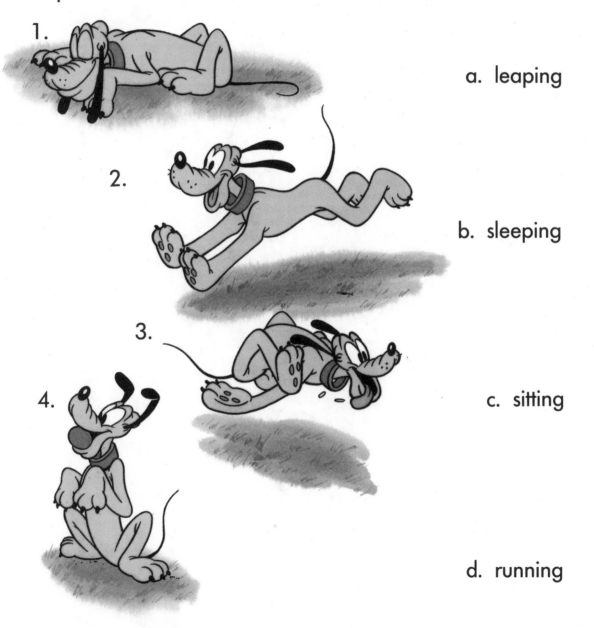

1.

2.

3.

4.

a. leaping

b. sleeping

c. sitting

d. running